RAGGEDY ANN'S NIGHTTIME RESCUE

By Eleanor Hudson
Based on a story by Johnny Gruelle

Illustrated by Judith Hunt

HAPPY HOUSE BOOKS
Random House, Inc.

Copyright © 1987 Macmillan, Inc. All rights reserved under International and Pan-American Copyright Conventions. Published in the United States by Random House, Inc., New York, and simultaneously in Canada by Random House of Canada Limited, Toronto. Based on "Raggedy Ann Rescues Fido" from *Raggedy Ann Stories* by Johnny Gruelle. The names and depictions of Raggedy Ann and of all related characters appearing herein are trademarks of Macmillan, Inc. ISBN: 0-394-88542-2
Manufactured in the United States of America   1 2 3 4 5 6 7 8 9 0

Marcella was a little girl who loved to play "school" with her dolls. This particular morning Raggedy Ann, her favorite doll, sat at the window watching to see if anyone was late for class. But all Raggedy Ann saw was Marcella's puppy dog, Fido, playing with a scruffy yellow puppy in the yard.

Suddenly Raggedy Ann's shoe button eyes grew wider. Fido and his friend were near a fence. As she watched, the two dogs wriggled through a hole and disappeared.

But Raggedy Ann did not say a word. For Marcella's dolls didn't want anyone to know that they could hear and speak.

By suppertime Marcella knew that something was wrong. It wasn't like Fido to stay away for a whole day. "He didn't even come home for his supper!" she said sadly, clutching Raggedy Ann and the Dutch doll.

"We'll find him," Mama comforted Marcella.

"If he's not home by tomorrow morning, I'll go look for him," Daddy said. "Now you must eat *your* supper, Marcella."

After Marcella had left the table, Raggedy Ann sighed from deep inside her soft, cottony stuffing. "There must be something we dolls can do," she thought.

That night the dolls lay in their beds and talked.
"Marcella was very sad at suppertime," said the Dutch doll.
"She misses her dog so much."
"I think we should show our love for Marcella by trying to

find Fido ourselves!" said Raggedy Ann. "He was playing with Priscilla's dog, Peterkins, this morning. That's our first clue."

"Let's not waste any time!" cried the tiny penny doll in a squeaky voice.

All the dolls jumped up from their beds and ran to the open window in the playroom. They helped each other up onto the window sill and then jumped to the soft grass below. *Plop!* Down they fell in all sorts of funny positions, but naturally the fall did not hurt them.

In a jiffy the dolls reached the hole in the fence. "Follow me," said the Indian doll. "I'll pick up the dogs' scent and we'll find out which way they went!"

The dolls trailed along behind the Indian doll and Raggedy Ann. Soon they arrived at Peterkins' doghouse, under the grape arbor in Priscilla's yard.

Peterkins was so surprised to see the little dolls coming up the path to his house!

"It's us, Marcella's dollies!" Raggedy Ann said to Peterkins. "We're very worried about Fido."

"Come in, come in," barked Peterkins. The dolls crowded into his doghouse and sat down.

"I'm worried too," Peterkins said. "Fido and I ran to the park and while we were playing a big man came running over. Fido thought he wanted to play with us. But he didn't! He scooped Fido up and put him in a wagon with a lot of other dogs!" Peterkins wiped his eyes with his paw. "I followed the wagon and saw the man put all the dogs in a big wire cage!"

"Poor Fido!" said Raggedy Ann. "That man must be the dogcatcher. He locks up dogs who are running loose. It's so sad for them to be away from their owners for even a day!" Raggedy Ann stamped her foot. "Come on, Peterkins, show us where the dogcatcher lives! We can rescue Fido ourselves—tonight!"

With the dolls pattering behind him, Peterkins led the way to the dogcatcher's yard. There were the captured dogs, whining softly in their cages. Poor Fido was muddy and wide-awake, and his ribbon was untied. He was very happy to see Peterkins and the dolls, and he ran right over to them.

"We'll try to get you out," Raggedy Ann whispered kindly.

"Hooray!" barked Fido as softly as he could.

Peterkins held Raggedy Ann gently in his mouth and stood up on his hind legs so she could raise the catch on the cage. Fido nudged open the gate, scampered out, and closed the gate behind him.

Some of the other dogs came over to see what was happening. "Take us, too!" they barked. Raggedy Ann shook her head.

"I'm sorry!" she said. "Your owners will come and get you very soon. The dogcatcher knows who they are from your dog tags. Tomorrow morning he'll tell them you're here."

Then Fido, Raggedy Ann, and the rest of the dolls followed Peterkins down the street.

Just as they reached the corner, the dogcatcher came out of his house to see why the dogs were making so much noise. He could hardly believe his eyes. Who were all those tiny little people running down the sidewalk?

"Must be some sort of ghosts," he muttered, and went back to bed.

"Thank you for helping us!" Raggedy Ann said to Peterkins once they were safely away from the dogcatcher's yard. Then the dolls trotted home after Fido just as the sun was beginning to rise.

"How will we get back into the playroom?" the Dutch doll asked anxiously. "We can't jump up that high!"

Raggedy Ann looked around. "Maybe we can use that old chair," she said.

With much huffing and
puffing, the dolls dragged
the chair over to the window
and managed to climb into
the playroom.

Fido followed them. He
was so tired that he crawled
into his basket and went
right to sleep.

"Oh, Fido!" Marcella cried the next morning when she came into the playroom. "You're home, safe and sound!"

"Yip, yip!" Fido jumped up and wagged his tail. Then he licked Raggedy Ann's face so hard that her smile would have disappeared if it hadn't been stitched on!